THIS CANDLEWICK BOOK BELONGS TO:

_____

_____

_____

_____

For David, Amelia,
Jane, Jason, and Lucy
with thanks.

Copyright © 1994 by Jez Alborough

All rights reserved.

First U.S. paperback edition 1996

The Library of Congress has cataloged the hardcover edition as follows:

Alborough, Jez.
It's the bear! / by Jez Alborough. — 1st U.S. ed.
Sequel to: Where's my teddy?
Summary: Eddie and his mom go into the woods for a picnic and
meet a very large, very hungry bear.
ISBN 1-56402-486-5 (hardcover)
[1. Bears—Fiction.   2. Picnicking—Fiction.   3. Stories in rhyme.]   I. Title.
PZ8.3.A33It   1995
[E]—dc20   94-10510

ISBN 1-56402-840-2 (paperback)

2 4 6 8 10 9 7 5 3 1

Printed in Hong Kong

This book was typeset in Garamond Light.
The pictures were done in watercolor, crayon, and pencil.

Candlewick Press
2067 Massachusetts Avenue
Cambridge, Massachusetts 02140

IT'S THE BEAR!

Jez Alborough

CANDLEWICK PRESS
CAMBRIDGE, MASSACHUSETTS

Eddie doesn't want to come
and picnic in the woods with Mom.

"I'm scared," he said, "about the bear,
the great big bear that lives in there."

"A bear?" said Mom. "That's silly, dear!
We don't get great big bears around here."

"There's just you and me and your teddy, Freddie.
Now let's all get the picnic ready."

"We've got lettuce,
tomatoes, and
cream cheese spread,
with hard-boiled eggs
and crusty brown bread.
There's orange juice,
cookies,
some chips and—

OH, MY!—

I've forgotten to pack
the blueberry pie . . . "

"I'll dash back and get it,"
she said. "Won't be long."
"BUT MOM!"
gasped Eddie . . .

too late—
SHE HAD GONE!

He sat on the basket
and tried not to cry.
Then . . .

"I CAN SMELL FOOD!"
yelled a voice
from nearby.

"*IT'S THE BEAR,*" cried Eddie. "*WHERE CAN I HIDE?*"

Then he opened the basket and clambered inside.

Out of the trees
stepped a big hungry bear,
licking his lips
and sniffing the air.
"A teddy bear's picnic,"
he bellowed. "Hooray!"
"Help," whispered Eddie.
"He's coming this way."

He cuddled
his teddy,
he huddled
and hid. . . .

Then a great big
bear bottom

sat down on the lid.

The bear munched
and he crunched.
He chomped
and he chewed,
and greedily gobbled up
all of the food.

"Eddie, I'm coming," called Mom. "Are you hurt?"
"It's the bear," cried Eddie. "He thinks I'm dessert!"

"A bear?" said Mom. "I told you, my dear.
Your Freddie's the only bear around here."

"I *TOLD* you!" cried Eddie.
"RUN!" shouted Mom.
"Blueberry pie," said the bear.
"I *LOVE* it . . ."